Singing the Dark

This book is for my mum, who taught me—among other things—to love nature.
—Gail

To Nathan, Fraser and Chelsea, and to the creative genius in all children.
—Sheena

Text copyright © 2001 by Gail, Sproule
Illustrations copyright © 2001 by Sheena Lott

Published in Canada by Fitzhenry & Whiteside, 195 Allstate Parkway, Markham, Ontario L3R 4T8
Published in the United States by Fitzhenry & Whiteside, 121 Harvard Avenue, Suite 2, Allston, Massachusetts 02134
Printed in Hong Kong

10 9 8 7 6 5 4 3 2 1

National Library of Canada Cataloguing in Publication Data

Sproule, Gail
Singing the dark

I. Lott, Sheena, 1950   II. Title.

PS8587.P759S55 2001   jC813'.54   C2001-901078-8
PZ7.S79694Si 2001

U.S. Cataloging-in-Publication Data
(Library of Congress Standards)

Sproule, Gail.
Singing the dark / written by Gail Sproule ; illustrated by Sheena Lott. –1st ed.
[32] p. : col. ill. ; cm.
Summary: As dusk falls, mother and child perform a bedtime ritual
by singing a welcoming song to the night.
IBSN 1-55041-6480
1. Bedtime -- Fiction. 2. Singing – Fiction.   3. Night – Fiction. I. Lott, Sheena, ill. II. Title.
[E] 21 2001 AC   CIP

Fitzhenry & Whiteside acknowledges with thanks the Canada Council for the Arts,
the Government of Canada through the Book Publishing Industry Development Program (BPIDP),
and the Ontario Arts Council for their support of our publishing program

Design by Wycliffe Smith

Singing
the Dark

By Gail Sproule

Illustrated by Sheena Lott

Fitzhenry & Whiteside

Sometimes, when the sun gets sleepy
and streaks red-golden rays across the sky,
Kaylie asks her mother, "Will you sing the dark
tonight?"

And her mother will sigh. "Tonight, Kaylie?"

Kaylie wiggles with hope, lights a smile
and says, "Please?"

Then her mother will stretch—arms
reaching, back arching—swoop down
and gather her girl for a hug.

Together they climb…

…the creaky wood stairs…

…which turn one way once…

…and then another again.

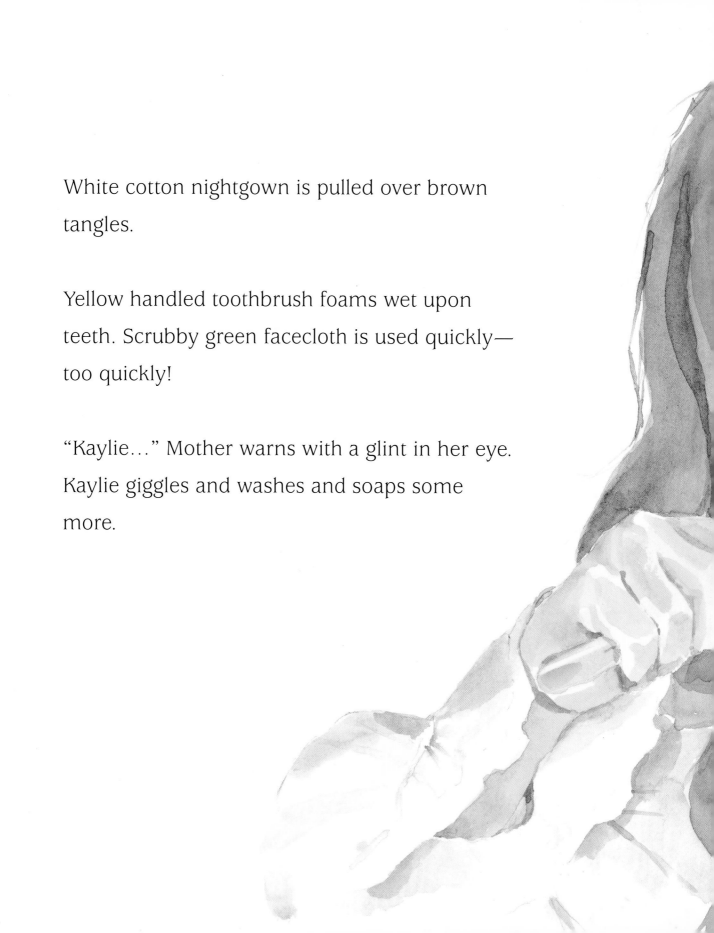

White cotton nightgown is pulled over brown tangles.

Yellow handled toothbrush foams wet upon teeth. Scrubby green facecloth is used quickly—too quickly!

"Kaylie…" Mother warns with a glint in her eye. Kaylie giggles and washes and soaps some more.

Taking bristly brush and slim, silver comb,
Kaylie fights with her hair until
it gives in and lies smooth.

The sky is now purple
and hazy and dim.

The crickets are singing,
Kerup! Kerup!
Kerup-up-up!

The screen door swishes, lets go with a bang,
and tippy-toe bare feet hurry! hurry!
over gravel:

"OUCH! EECH! EECH! OUCH!"

They walk hand in hand—one shadow big,
the other one small.

Then two become one, outlines stretching
and melting together.

"Dusk is now here. Feel the dew
on the grass?"

"Oh yes!" Kaylie says with a hop and a step,
for the grass is squishy and wet between her toes.

In the middle of the yard, they stop and
stand still. Starting low, humming soft,
Kaylie's mother now sings.
Calling warm, velvet darkness…
…to blanket the ground…
…making day things sleepy…
…and wakening the night.

By the stone step at the edge
of the garden, flowers are
closing and colors
are fading.

Kaylie stands quiet,
but tingles all over,
listening while Mother
calls the dark to emerge.

Sunset glow dims and
darkness approaches,
but the jewels of the night—
first one, then another—
wink into life.

Now Kaylie sings too, a soft little murmur,
greeting the wish-makers
high in the sky.

Two voices are rising, one big and one small, to welcome the coming of a dark summer's night.

Shadows spill forth like ink from a pen,
but silver-lit moon slides light through the trees.

Birds are tucked cosy and warm in their nests,
but the bats are delighted, as night time is flight
time for creatures like them.

A cool little breeze comes to ruffle and play...

...brings goosebumps and shivers...

...and sweet scents...

...of night blooming flowers.

Voices are falling, trailing off with a yawn, and
Mother's arms form a circle, making a hug.

Kaylie is snuggling, feeling tired, near sleep…
and singing the dark is now complete.

"Enough?" Mother asks
with a squeeze and a smile.

"Enough for tonight," Kaylie agrees
with a laugh. "But you know...the dark
will need singing tomorrow."